Click

PRAISE FOR *STORYSHARES*

"One of the brightest innovators and game-changers in the education industry."
– Forbes

"Your success in applying research-validated practices to promote literacy serves as a valuable model for other organizations seeking to create evidence-based literacy programs."

- Library of Congress

"We need powerful social and educational innovation, and Storyshares is breaking new ground. The organization addresses critical problems facing our students and teachers. I am excited about the strategies it brings to the collective work of making sure every student has an equal chance in life."
– Teach For America

"Around the world, this is one of the up-and-coming trailblazers changing the landscape of literacy and education."
- International Literacy Association

"It's the perfect idea. There's really nothing like this. I mean wow, this will be a wonderful experience for young people."   - Andrea Davis Pinkney, Executive Director, Scholastic

"Reading for meaning opens opportunities for a lifetime of learning. Providing emerging readers with engaging texts that are designed to offer both challenges and support for each individual will improve their lives for years to come. Storyshares is a wonderful start."
- David Rose, Co-founder of CAST & UDL

Click

Sophie Rathmann

STORYSHARES

Story Share, Inc.
New York. Boston. Philadelphia.

Storyshares
Story Share, Inc.
24 N. Bryn Mawr Avenue #340
Bryn Mawr, PA 19010-3304
www.storyshares.org

Inspiring reading with a new kind of book.

Interest Level: High School
Grade Level Equivalent: 4.1

9781642615876

Book design by Storyshares

Printed in the United States of America

Storyshares Presents

1

Gwen drove home from the last day of school to find that her dad had already finished packing the truck. It sat in the driveway, the truck's bed popped open and the keys in the front seat. She drove into the garage and got out of her beat-up Subaru, slamming the door shut. Both cars were covered in a layer of dust. Gwen considered this a testament to the fact that she and her father lived in the middle of nowhere, where dirt roads still existed.

Gwen frowned as she hauled her bag out of the trunk. She made sure not to crush the expensive camera hanging around her neck. For God's sake, couldn't she have one day to relax before Malcolm threw her onto some random mountain? Hadn't he promised her that? She glared at the fully packed car. Damn him.

Gwen didn't doubt that Malcolm knew exactly what he'd promised. But Malcolm had never really been one to heed his daughter's wishes—especially not over the summer.

Gwen let out a long sigh of frustration, then kicked open the bent screen door and stomped inside. She plodded through the mudroom without taking off her shoes. She slammed her backpack down in the kitchen loudly to notify Malcolm that she was home.

"I didn't get any C's!" she shouted into the empty air.

"Congrats," came the dry, semi-sarcastic reply. Malcolm's boots became visible on the stairs. "You've got your bag ready?"

As his face came into view, Gwen directed her most scathing glare in his direction. Normally, it worked. Despite her short stature, she was an intimidating young woman. But her glares had never really worked on him.

Malcolm paused, his shaggy dark gray hair framed his cheekbones. He raised a grizzled brow at her. "What?"

"I didn't get any C's," she said again.

"Well, you still suck at negotiating," he said. "I know you asked for a week off this summer, but you forgot to specify *when* you wanted the week off." He brushed past her to get to the fridge. When he opened it, she saw that he'd already cleaned it out. "I thought I taught you to think more carefully about your words."

Gwen bit her tongue and shook her head. She wished she could blow her top at him, but she knew that wouldn't change anything.

"Well, *Malcolm,* not everything is a hostage negotiation. I thought I was clear enough."

He threw a glance her way when she used his proper name but shrugged off her icy tone. "Yeah, well, you're not a princess, so buck up and take the lesson. You have your bag ready?"

Without a word, Gwen picked up her backpack and left the kitchen. Who was he kidding? She always had a bag ready. That was one of the first lessons she'd learned.

She snapped one last photo of the bright white light filtering through her bedroom window, reflecting off a bare canvas she had yet to paint. Then she grabbed her bag and left.

* * *

When they pulled into a motel parking lot at two in the morning, Gwen was floored. Normally, they'd leave civilization completely behind as soon as they got in the truck. In fact, she'd powered off her phone and handed it over to Malcolm hours ago.

"Why are we stopping?" she asked blearily.

Malcolm shook his head and rubbed a hand over his face. "Migraine," he said with a grimace.

Gwen put out a hand. "Gimme the wallet. I'll take care of the room."

Malcolm slapped the beat-up wallet solidly into her palm and buried his face in his hands, groaning.

Gwen got out of the car and stretched, slightly worried. The truth was Malcolm was getting old. They both knew it. His joints gave him more trouble, his migraines had gotten more frequent, and he could feel every storm approaching in his bones.

At least he'd been sober for three years. That, more than anything, kept her hopeful.

She booked the room, went back to the car, and dragged Malcolm inside. She forced him to drink a glass of water and take some medicine before allowing him to sleep. He grumbled his way through it all. He distrusted medicine, but Gwen watched him down the pills anyway. Then she got him into one of the beds.

She wondered how long he'd been on the road, waiting and feeling his migraine get worse but not waking her up. Something in her stomach sank. Malcolm was no father of the year, but damn it, he tried—especially now.

* * *

Gwen got her camera out of the car when she was sure that Malcolm was asleep. She spent a few minutes in the yellow-lit, slightly misty parking lot of the motel. She wanted to take a few good shots of the car in the eerie light. Maybe she'd make a photo series of the trip for her art portfolio.

The air outside was crisp and clear. She could hear the crickets chirping. When she finally got cold and started feeling weirded out by the empty parking lot and looming mist, she crept back into the room. As she turned on the bathroom light to brush her teeth, a thin strip of light fell across Malcolm's face. His features were smoothed out in a way they rarely were when he was awake.

Gwen instinctually raised the camera and clicked the shutter. For a moment, she was still. Then she sighed and removed the camera from her neck.

2

Gwen woke up before Malcolm the next morning. She snuck quietly out of the room to get some food from the motel's complimentary breakfast. She got a bagel and some tea and brought Malcolm black coffee and a bagel of his own.

He woke up the way he always did. He shifted, and his breathing changed. His eyes fluttered and then, quite suddenly, they were wide open. He sat straight up, running a hand through his hair and hastily throwing off the blankets. He squinted at Gwen as he picked up the coffee from the table.

"You're up early."

She shrugged. "Learned from the best, I guess. And I slept a lot in the car."

Malcolm grunted, possibly in agreement, and continued to drink his coffee. Then, in a motion she almost missed, Malcolm tossed something small in her direction.

Mostly on instinct, Gwen snatched the shiny thing out of the air. Her stomach flipped over in shock and excitement. He'd tossed her the car keys.

She looked up at him, somewhat awestruck. He'd never let her drive on a trip before. Hell, he usually never told her where they were *going*.

He gave her a wry smile. "Wanna drive a leg of the trip?"

"Really?" she breathed, turning the key over in her hand. It was like being handed a sacred relic—the keys to Malcolm's truck.

"Figure you're old enough. It's about time," he said gruffly, shrugging.

Gwen pressed her free hand to her mouth. She wondered why he suddenly thought she was ready. She sure hadn't earned the privilege, especially not with her whole attitude towards the trip. So why?

Malcolm finished the coffee, chucked it in the bin, and made his way into the bathroom. Gwen, still in awe, slowly raised the camera. Light peered through the half-closed shutters. She took a picture of it falling across her open palm and the beaten-up keys. The angle was perfect. The keys looked fiery gold-orange. Even the dust motes in the air were visible.

* * *

"So, where are we headed?" she asked as they got back on the interstate.

"Bottom of Idaho. Murphy Hot Springs."

Gwen nearly snapped her neck as she turned to look at him. "We're doing the Idaho Centennial?"

He nodded firmly. "You're ready for it."

Gwen's stomach turned over, partly in excitement and partly in fear. The Idaho Centennial Trail was 900 miles long. Only ten people had ever completed the full trail. It would take about 52 days—almost all of summer break.

"I want to re-check all our supplies when we get there."

Malcolm nodded and smiled as he looked out the window.

Gwen bit her lip. Had Malcolm arranged checkpoints? He must have—they'd never be able to carry enough food, and she wasn't about to make that mistake again. Maybe it was a test. If they ate less than 3,000 calories a day, they were going to start losing weight. In fact, they might even need 4,000 a day, just to be safe.

She glanced at Malcolm. Was he going to let her use a calculator?

* * *

Gwen repacked her bag three times in the trailhead parking lot before she was sure that she was ready. But then Malcolm surprised her.

"I've got one more thing to get," he said. He set his pack on the tarp that Gwen had laid out.

Gwen tightened her ponytail and looked up at him in surprise. "We're not missing anything, I checked." In fact, she'd checked the food over so carefully she was pretty sure she could list everything they were carrying by memory.

He looked off into the distance, flipping the car keys through his fingers. "I know." There was a long silence as the wind tore at their clothing and packs. "I won't be long."

Still, when he got into the car and drove away, Gwen's stomach tightened. Where the hell was he going? What would she do if he didn't come back?

It was an irrational fear—she had all the food for the first leg of the journey. But she looked into the little valley, with its small town and beat-up houses, and wondered if they were friendly to strangers.

He'd be back, she told herself. He always came back.

Click

3

The deep blue truck pulled up just as the sun was beginning to set. Gwen could feel the muscles in her shoulders loosening up. Her curiosity was back in full force but so was her suspicion. If he'd just gone and gotten drunk, this was going to be hell. But his driving hadn't seemed impaired.

She looked at his face through the windshield, surprised to see a small smile drifting over his lips. She lifted the camera from where it hung around her neck and focused on the reflection of the darkening sky in the windshield. She held her breath and clicked the shutter.

He opened the door and went around to the passenger side. Gwen watched in confusion as a small, light-colored thing bobbed in and out of sight. Then, on the other side of the car, four paws hit the ground.

Gwen gasped and leapt to her feet as Malcolm made his way around the truck. He was guiding the well-behaved dog by an army-green leash. Malcolm looked satisfied.

Gwen bent down to let the dog sniff her. She rubbed its ears. She'd wanted a dog for *ages . . .* but to walk the trail?

She looked up at Malcolm. "Where'd you get him?"

Malcolm smiled. "Bought him last year as a puppy. Went up for a week to make sure his training was alright and then went back this March to make sure he still remembered everything. You remember those trips, right?" He looked down at the dog.

Gwen remembered. Malcolm had a habit of disappearing on long trips. It was part of his work often enough, and she'd gotten used to it. Still, it scared her every time. It left so much of his time unaccounted for. To know he'd spent a week each year training a dog relieved her.

If there was one thing Malcolm was made for, it was training animals. He spoke their language. They had some kind of connection Gwen didn't yet understand, but she hoped to someday.

She thought back to the barn and horse arena Malcolm had built behind their house. She'd watched him take in horse after horse, usually broken, pathetic, skinny little things. And she'd watch him retrain them. He'd turn them back into trusting creatures with gleaming coats before finding them the perfect new owner.

That was what he did at the end of every summer—find a few rough "projects" to adopt and love and train. She'd watched him at five in the morning, delivering a colt. She'd seen him standing nose to nose with a horse that everyone else had called "vicious," talking quietly to it as the sun rose.

To know that he'd trained the dog was something special.

"He's coming on the hike?"

Malcolm shrugged. "That's up to you. If he comes, I want you to take care of him. Make sure he eats, has water, stays nearby. I've trained him well enough, but you've got the choice. And if you do well, we'll keep him."

Gwen could already feel the responsibility of the dog settling onto her shoulders like a weight. But she'd wanted a dog for so long . . .

She nodded. "What's his name?"

Malcolm's smile split into a grin.

* * *

Zim was extraordinarily well trained. By the seventh day, Gwen was surprised at how routine taking care of the dog had become. He was young and full of energy, but he was sweet. He was a good distraction from the difficulties of the hike.

At first her feet were in a lot of pain, and her legs were burning and sore. It took a few days to adjust to the pace of almost 25 miles per day. But one week in, and she was past the worst of it. She had, so far, done an excellent job navigating.

She looked up at the sun, which was beginning to set. Just as she was about to open her mouth, Malcolm said, "Let's pull off the trail. That little ridge up there seems like a nice shelter."

Gwen gave him a thumbs up and whistled. Zim came bounding into sight. That night, as they sat by the fire, Gwen took her camera out of her bag and took a picture of Malcolm petting Zim. They were both illuminated by the flickering orange-red flames. The desert landscape was just barely visible in the shadows behind them, more of a suggestion than a concrete detail.

Malcolm shot her an uneasy glance, and she lowered the lens. But he didn't say anything. Carefully, she kept the angle and pointed the camera into the flames. But she couldn't bring herself to waste the film, so she didn't take the shot.

Click

4

The transition into the mountains was gradual. Soon the grass thickened, and the trees became more frequent. Other signs of vegetation and life were everywhere. As Gwen stood on a butte and watched thunderclouds roll in, her hair blew crazily around her face. The dark curls obscured her vision before being blown in new directions.

She looked behind her and snapped her fingers, pointing back at Malcolm halfway down the hill. Instantly, Zim shot off to go retrieve him. Gwen picked up her camera and adjusted the settings, making sure the stormy gray-blues of the sky contrasted with the deep, vibrant greens.

As Zim circled around Malcolm, they both looked up the hill. Gwen clicked the shutter just as a peal of thunder cracked overhead.

Seconds later, it began to rain.

* * *

It was late that evening when the weather had cleared. But because they'd stopped early, neither Malcolm nor Gwen were tired.

Gwen pointed up at Orion. "Hey, I always liked that story as a kid. You're good at telling it."

Malcolm smiled softly. "I've always loved telling stories, I guess. But go ahead, you tell it tonight. Let's see what you remember."

Gwen took a few moments before she began, searching for the proper starting point. Then she let the story unfold, and it came out naturally. It was almost as if she was watching someone else tell it—she barely had to think.

When she stopped, Malcolm wiped his eyes. Gwen kindly pretended not to see him do it. The silence stretched out, and Zim shifted where he lay against her leg.

"Hey, Dad?" she asked because maybe he was in the right mood to tell the story. "Can you tell me about mom again?"

He blinked at her and shifted, then looked back up at the stars. "Ah. Which part of that story do you want?" he asked carefully.

"What was the best part?" Gwen asked, looking down at her arms. Her skin was the biggest connection she had to her mother—she had faint vitiligo markings that wound their way all across her skin. But she'd never even once seen a photo of the woman. Malcolm didn't have any.

"Let's see," Malcolm began, "your mother was a very strong woman. Not in the physical sense, but she carried herself in a way that let other people know she was a force to be reckoned with. Like you, actually. You remind me of her, and you look more like her every day."

Gwen was quiet, watching the stars. She felt strangely sad and proud at the same time.

"Anyway," Malcolm continued, "there was a time in your life when your mother, me, and a couple of our closest friends went on a trip. We were backpacking from place to place. And we'd just arrived in this tiny little place, exhausted. Truthfully, I'm not even sure where we were.

"We found this beat-up little inn. We all crammed inside, and a great storm started up outside. The rain came down in buckets, and the thunder crashed. It felt like gods were outside, angry and fighting.

"The owner of that little inn knew what was happening though. He started moving everything he could upstairs. He was stacking furniture and the like. I didn't believe him when he said it was going to flood, but your mom knew right away that he was right. Soon enough, we all pitched in.

"That was one hell of a night because of course it flooded. We looked outside and everything, just all of it, was underwater."

Malcolm shook his head, his hands telling the story with him. "The next morning, that innkeeper pulled out some canoes he had in his garage. We took turns going out into the village and making sure everyone was alright. Except your mom, of course. She stayed in that canoe all day. She went all over town and brought back people who needed shelter. She was just a force of nature in her own way."

His voice became quiet. "Anyway, we stayed until the water went down and another week after that." Then Malcolm was silent.

Gwen had never heard the story before. Slowly, she turned on the flash of the camera, then she put her hand up in front of the lens. She pulled up her sleeve so that the lines on her skin were visible. Holding her hand out like she was reaching into the stars, she took the photo.

Malcolm let the moment extend for a few more seconds before he asked, "Where's the North Star tonight?"

Gwen knew he knew the answer because this was the whole point of knowing the stars.

"There," she said, pointing.

Then she rattled off the cardinal directions and the approximate date based on the position. Quietly, she added in the actual date, too, because she was still keeping track of their next checkpoint.

5

The mornings got colder after the middle of their hike. Gwen had added more calories at their last checkpoint, so their packs were heavy once again. Still, Malcolm nodded in approval when she handed him the Camas flowers. He checked to make sure she'd picked the right ones, then began munching on the bright blue plant. "Good eye."

Gwen nodded and chewed her own handful, starting with the fireweed.

"When did you review the plants in the region?"

Gwen shook her head. "I didn't. I just remembered." Instantly, she felt a sinking feeling. "How many others have I missed?" She held up a hand. "I know I missed the Oregon grapes and maybe the mint."

Malcolm nodded. "You did. And you missed rose, cattails, yarrow, elk's thistle, and some wild strawberries."

Gwen clenched her teeth. The roses should have been obvious, at least. But . . . "If there's any way you think I'm picking thistles, think again, old man."

He chuckled and pointed into the distance. "Two fingers from that big rock, there's a yellow bird."

Gwen swung her camera up, measured the distance with her fingers, and found the bird perched lightly on a branch. Malcolm liked birds. This was a townsend's warbler, if she remembered the description right. Malcolm had said it looked like a zebra lemon. She took the photo for him.

"Townsend's warbler?"

He gave her an impressed look and nodded. "If only you remembered plants like that."

Gwen gestured to the woods around them. "C'mon. Help me review, if it means so much."

A real smile touched his lips. "Thatta-way, princess."

* * *

By the time they were three-quarters of the way through the hike, Gwen had almost forgotten there was a world outside of the trail. She knew this was Malcolm's way of preparing her for something. She'd proved to him by now that she could handle the responsibility of leading the hike and caring for the dog, but this summer it was more than that. It was more than just a hike, more than just survival skills.

There had always been something between them, but she had let it fade when she started growing up. Now it was coming back. Maybe it was partly the dog, but it was also the stories Malcolm began to tell. They weren't all real. In fact, many of them were myths and fairytales. But there was something important in them, so Gwen listened.

Sometimes, when the moment seemed right, she pulled old stories from childhood and dusted them off. She'd tell them to Malcolm and watch for his reaction. She was careful about telling them because there was something almost criminal about messing them up.

Sometimes, she didn't like the stories, or they didn't make sense, but they were good stories anyway. It was similar to the frustration of checking supplies over at every checkpoint and realizing every ounce counted.

They were getting farther and farther north. There were patches of snow in the mountains despite the fact that it was summer. They had also been in the forest for several days now. But as Gwen rounded the corner, she spotted the top of the slope. It was wide and open and filled with wildflowers.

"Malcolm!" she called, spinning around on the trail to face him.

His head snapped up. "What?"

She pointed, and he smiled. She took off running, laughing as Zim bounded next to her. She played with him in the open grass, under the robin's-egg-blue shell of the sky.

When she looked up, Malcolm was crouched in the field a few feet away, cradling a brilliant purple flower in his palms. Gwen raised her camera and focused on his hands and the flower. She let the rest—the green grass, his tan cargo pants, the red of his bag—fade into the background. The yellow flowers scattered behind him contrasted with the purple, even when they weren't in focus. The sky was perfect and clear.

She clicked the shutter.

Click

6

When Gwen went back to school, she stayed after on the first day. She placed her photos on the proper paper and painstakingly developed them. The next day, she passed around her portfolio.

On the top was the washed-out photo of her room, with the white curtains and empty canvas. Then the yellow of the lights reflected in the motel parking lot. Then the orange-gold of the car keys in her hand, followed by the blue of the truck and the sky reflected in the windshield.

The campfire in the desert was next, with its deep shadows and red overtones. In sharp contrast, the green butte followed it. The last two photos seemed like opposites. Her hand, reaching into the night sky, alone in black and white. And then Malcolm's dirty hands, with bright purple in the middle and every other color bursting in the background.

Remembering these tender moments that she captured, Gwen found herself looking forward to her next trip with Malcolm.

About The Author

Sophie Rathmann is a young author currently attending Brandeis University. Her passions are centered around English, education, art, and horseback riding. She enjoys all forms of nerd culture and has a love affair with food of all kinds.

About The Publisher

Story Shares is a nonprofit focused on supporting the millions of teens and adults who struggle with reading by creating a new shelf in the library specifically for them. The ever-growing collection features content that is compelling and culturally relevant for teens and adults, yet still readable at a range of lower reading levels.

Story Shares generates content by engaging deeply with writers, bringing together a community to create this new kind of book. With more intriguing and approachable stories to choose from, the teens and adults who have fallen behind are improving their skills and beginning to discover the joy of reading. For more information, visit storyshares.org.

Easy to Read. Hard to Put Down.

www.ingramcontent.com/pod-product-compliance
Lightning Source LLC
Chambersburg PA
CBHW071228170626
46809CB00005BA/1980